ARD

MW01136647

Table of Contents

Chapter 1

Heather had found herself in plenty of uncomfortable situations before. While investigating cases, she had been shot at, chased and poisoned. However, as she squeezed and struggled to pull herself into a potential bridesmaid dress, she felt hard-pressed to think of a time she had ever felt more uncomfortable. The dress was tight where it should have been loose and loose where it should have been tight. It also didn't help that the dress was a bright fluorescent orange that clashed horribly with her red hair.

Heather waddled because that's how the dress forced her to

move, to the dressing room door. She thought to herself that she better not have to chase any criminals in a dress like this. However, she put a false smile on as she moved into the lobby-like area of the changing rooms. It was all about the future bride Mona today. If there was even a chance that Mona would like this dress, then she had better practice grinning-and-bearing-it. As Heather caught more reflections on herself in the semi-circle mirror display, she thought to herself that it was more likely that her dog Dave would sit up on a piano stool and play Beethoven's 5th Symphony than Mona would like the look of this dress on her Maid of Honor.

She accidentally allowed a frown to fall across her face as she checked how the dress looked from behind. She was thinking that it would be impossible to find an uglier dress when she was joined by the co-Maid-of-Honor and her best friend, Amy.

Amy usually looked nice in anything she wore, but this dress was certainly trying to make her look ridiculous. The teal color was pretty, but it was made entirely of ruffles that were threatening to engulf her.

"I need more of that champagne," Amy grumbled.
Heather laughed, and the two of them did take a glass of the

complimentary bubbly. Amy suggested a toast, "To Maids of Honor truly willing to do anything for the bride."

Heather let her glass clink against her bestie's and they both took a sip.

"Of course, Mona would never actually choose one of these dresses," Heather said.

"I don't know why we even came to this boutique," Amy said. "It's not like we're going to buy anything here."

Heather nodded but soon had to retract that nod. Mona Petrov emerged from her dressing stall in a wedding dress that could only be described as magical. With Mona's dark hair and beautiful eyes, she probably would love lovely wearing a burlap sack, but there was something about this dress that made it special. They could tell right away that this was "the one."

"I feel like a princess," Mona said. She gave a little twirl as she joined them to let the fabric swirl around her. "I'd be able to dance in this too."

"I have to admit," Heather said. "I think we're going to have trouble finding a dress that's better than this. It looks perfect."

"It feels perfect," Mona said, practically glowing with happiness.

"How lucky can you be?" Amy asked. "The first dress you try on is the right one."

"I wasn't so lucky with husbands," Mona reminded them. "But I know that Col is the right man for me. My true love. And having something go right with wedding plans is such a relief. I was starting to think that our marriage wasn't meant to be."

"You're both madly in love with each other," Heather said. "Of course, it's meant to be."

"You do look like a princess," Amy said, focusing on what she said when she joined them instead of the mushy stuff about true love. "But, right now, we are your lowly peasants." She touched a ruffle that was as large as her hand. "Or maybe your jesters right now."

"They're not that bad," Mona said.

They were about to protest with Heather suggesting that Mona's joy from her own dress might be clouding her judgment and Amy using stronger language when they were joined by the owner of the boutique. Sheila Lordlittle was an overpowering woman. She had long graying hair pulled back into a pony tail, and wore all black. When they had entered the shop, Amy had joked that she looked more ready for a funeral than a wedding. Sheila Lordlittle had responded that she was an artiste.

"Mona, my dear, dear Mona," said Sheila Lordlittle. "This dress was made for you. And as the one who makes all these dresses, I can say that with certainty."

"You make all these dresses?" Amy asked, comparing the difference between the wedding dress and the bridesmaid dresses.

"I design them all, yes," said Sheila Lordlittle. "My assistants do help with the sewing. Abigail! Ollie!"

The two assistants ran into the room. They were both also all in black and had a look of slight fear.

"Do we need to call the police again?" Ollie asked. He had perfectly styled hair and looked ready to bring out his cell phone.

"No, not at all," his boss told him. "I just wanted to show off that all our work is handcrafted."

Abigail showed off her hands to the group.

"Don't be smart," Sheila Lordlittle said. "Now I believe this lovely bride here would like this dress. Would you get the veil to match it?"

Her assistants agreed and left together. Sheila Lordlittle was about to compliment Mona more to make sure she secured the sale, when Heather asked, "Why did you need to call the police?"

"Oh, a trifling matter," Sheila Lordlittle said with a shrug. "A customer was unhappy with a dress. All I can say is that I am not responsible for the bodies that visit this shop. Certain styles will look better on certain brides. They can listen to me or not. All I am responsible for is assuring you that every dress here is one of a kind. No other wedding party will have the exact same look as you."

"I should hope not," said Amy.

Sheila Lordlittle decided to take that as a compliment. "And now this wedding dress is a definite. But which of these bridesmaid dresses do you want?"

Heather and Amy exchanged a look as Mona seemed to really consider the options. Finally, she put them out of their misery by asking, "Do you have anything in pink? I've been considering having pink roses at my ceremony."

Abigail and Ollie returned with the veil, and then Sheila Lordlittle sent them off again to look for more bridesmaid dresses. Heather wanted to let out a sigh of relief was but starting to find the dress too tight to exhale or inhale deeply.

Sheila Lordlittle put the veil on Mona so that it flowed down her back, and Heather's thoughts about her own uncomfortableness disappeared. She felt only joy for her friend.

"I feel like a bride," Mona said. Happy tears started to form in her eyes.

"I'm glad this is working out for her," Amy whispered to her friend. "Because I feel like I'd rather be facing a crazed killer than wear this dress any longer."

"Be careful what you wish for," Heather joked back.

Chapter 2

"You two really are the best co-Maids-of-Honor that a girl could ask for," Mona said.

"And you say that before we provide you with donuts," Heather said with a smile.

After a morning full of trying on dresses, they had come to Donut Delights to have a snack and relax. Since Mona had found her dress so early, she had been able to recline on a couch with champagne as her friends put on a fashion show of potential bridesmaid dresses. Sometimes it felt like a comedy show more than a fashion show. In the end, they had not found a dress that Mona liked. Both Heather and Amy were grateful that she hadn't selected some of the unusual choices.

"I wonder if that's done on purpose," Amy said. "Make the bridesmaids look terrible, so the bride looks better."

"It might be because she has every dress is one of a kind," Heather said. "Maybe she started to run out of ideas after being open for so long."

"All I know," said Amy. "Is that I would rather have my bridesmaids in a dress that another wedding somewhere wore than to have them in a dress with a squirrel tail like that one I tried on."

"I'd have to be nuts to pick that one," Mona joked.

They groaned and laughed, and Heather decided it was time to bring out the donuts.

"What flavor is it this week?" Mona asked. Mona was a fan of the new flavors of the week both as a friend and as a business ally. Mona's fiancé was Col Owen of Owen's Tea Shop, Heather's joint venture partner. Thanks to their working together, Heather was able to see Donut Delights' business expand. Recently their online orders had really been picking up steam; so much so, that a new investor was trying to convince her to open up another location in Florida.

"This has been a stressful time," Heather said. She had been finding the decision to move a big and stressful one but wasn't ready to hear all her friends' reactions to it yet. Instead, she focused on wedding plans. "Wedding planning can be stressful, so I thought we needed something most women love as a tension reliever. I'd like to introduce the Chocolate Chocolate Donut."

"Delicious, delicious," said Amy.

"I do like the sound of that," said Mona.

"I bet we'll like the taste even better," Amy said.

Heather delivered a plate of the new donuts on their table, and the women appreciated the smell of the freshly baked donuts.

"This looks more like a Chocolate, Chocolate, Chocolate, Chocolate Donut," Amy said.

Heather laughed. "Yes, there are more than two parts of the donut that are chocolate. But I think that name would take too long for customers to say when ordering."

"It might hold up the line," Amy agreed. "Because a lot of people would still order them."

"The Chocolate Chocolate Donut name comes from combining dark chocolate and milk chocolate flavors into the donut. It has a dark chocolate inspired cake base, so it is rich and a little more savory. Then it is filled with a milk chocolate inspired center for sweetness. The icing on top is also chocolate. And I could resist adding some mini chocolate chips on top," said Heather.

"I can't resist taking a bite," Amy said, and then she did. The other ladies joined her and smiled as they enjoyed the chocolate flavors mixing together in their mouths.

"I wish I had never tried this," Mona said suddenly.

Heather was concerned for a moment. Had she miscalculated in her recipe? Was she receiving a complaint?

"Because," Mona said. "I'm going to want to keep eating these and I have a wedding dress I'm going to have to fit into."

They all laughed.

Then Mona said to Heather, "I do really want to thank you for everything. I know you can get really busy with your shop, and sleuthing and raising a family." She turned to Amy and continued, "And with your sleuthing too, and moving into a new house."

Amy nodded but didn't comment. She and her boyfriend had just moved into a new house, but after their landlord's recent murder they weren't sure how long they would be able to stay there. They were still waiting to hear what the family that would inherit the house planned to do with it.

"Thank you for taking the time to help me with my dream wedding," said Mona.

"That's what the job of Maids of Honor is for," Heather assured her.

"We take this very seriously," said Amy.

"I know," said Mona, "but I still appreciate it."

"We will always make time for you," Heather said. "You're our friend, and we want this wedding to be as perfect as you do. Don't you worry about that."

She was about to recommend seconds on donuts before they started deciding on table settings (luckily cake tasting was another day so they could enjoy as many donuts as they wanted) when someone joined them at their table.

Rudolph Rodney tipped a hat towards them and gave them his greetings.

"How is this fine day treating you, ladies? With delicious donuts in front of you, I can imagine it is going rather well," he said.

They agreed that they had been having a nice day and told him about the new Chocolate Chocolate Donut.

"That does sound wonderful and probably worth double the compliments," he said. "I hope you've been seriously considering my offer to start a Donut Delights in Key West. Now that I've been thinking about it, I don't think I could stand to return there without knowing I could get these fresh donuts there every week."

"You could order them online," Amy said, making her feelings towards a potential move known. "Like other out-of-towners do."

"What's this about Key West?" asked Mona.

"I've made Heather a splendid offer about opening a second shop in one of my properties in Key West. It'd be a prime location, and I know it would do well. I'm even bribing her with one of my housing properties," Rudolph Rodney said. "But she seems to be dragging her feet."

"So, you'd have to move?" Mona asked.

"This is all just an idea," Heather said. "If I became serious about it I'd, of course, have to talk to Col about it. He is my joint venture partner. And I wouldn't just abandon your wedding."

Rudolph Rodney seemed to sense that he had created some tension at the table and decided to depart gracefully. "I think I'll just go and order my donuts now.

I'm picking some up for my nephew Roadkill and myself. I'm visiting him this afternoon. So nice seeing you all."

He left, and the women continued their wedding planning with less enthusiasm than before. Heather thought that he couldn't have come at a worse time if he planned it.

Chapter 3

That night Heather set the table, grateful that her husband Ryan had picked up dinner on his way home from work. They both had some annoying information to share and were updating each other on their days.

Ryan was between cases at the Hillside Police Force, but there was still a mystery to be solved at headquarters.

"I don't understand why they're giving Hoskins credit for a case that we solved," Ryan frowned.

Heather rolled her eyes. Ryan's partner Detective Hoskins had proven to be an inept investigator on many cases. He was much better at finding candy to snack on than finding clues at a crime scene. However, on their last case, he had been the shoulder to cry on for a woman who had just lost her father. It turned out the woman worked for the mayor and was now praising Hoskins's police work.

"I guess the victim's daughter has a lot of sway in town," Heather shrugged.

"But did the chief forget all the times that Hoskins left chocolate fingerprints on evidence folders?" Ryan asked.

"I might leave chocolate prints places sometimes," Heather said. "But I'm always cognizant of when it could affect an investigation."

"If they're fingerprints because you're making those Chocolate Chocolate Donuts, then you are forgiven," Ryan said. "I know I shouldn't let this Hoskins thing bother me. As long as a case gets solved and a killer is off the streets, it shouldn't matter who gets a pat on the back from the town."

"I understand why it bothers you. It bothers me too," said Heather. "And we have to be careful if we tell Amy because it will bother her so much that she might go yell at City Hall."

Ryan laughed.

"I can give you a pat on the back," Heather said. "A lot of murderers have been stopped because of you, Shepherd."

"I can say the same about you, Shepherd." He smiled back. He thought about it and then said, "Getting away from Hoskins could be a positive reason for moving to Key West. Though would we be afraid to leave Hillside in his hands?"

"I don't even want to talk about a move or Key West tonight," Heather said.

"Oh," said Ryan. "Is it bad to bring up that being inspired by our talk about the location, I picked up a dinner with a tropical theme? Shrimp and fish."

"No. That makes picking up dinner even sweeter," she said.

"Why don't you want to think about it tonight?"

"It's just that Rudolph Rodney tried to talk to me about it at Donut Delights today right in front of Amy and Mona. You should have seen Mona's face when she thought I was going to bail on her wedding. And Amy is decidedly against our moving."

"I know it's hard. But we can't let our friends dictate our lives. We're going to have to decide what is best for our family," Ryan said.

"I know," Heather said, as they began to set the food on the table.

"How are you feeling about it right now?"

"I'm not sure," Heather said. "If I was against it, I'm sure I would have told Rudolph Rodney no right away. I'm intrigued by the offer. But it is a big change. I'd miss everyone. Still, part of me wants to run with the opportunity and see where Donut Delights can take me."

"I think I feel the same. Ever since we talked about, I've been thinking about how exciting a new city could be for us. I also wouldn't mind being near the beach," Ryan said.

"We probably should sit down with Rudolph Rodney and get some more details," Heather said. "But he shouldn't talk about it in front of our friends until we have a firmer idea about what we're feeling. We haven't even talked to Lilly about it."

"Talked to me about what?" Lilly asked, entering with the family pets. Dave, the dog, seemed to sense that secrets were being kept and began sniffing to figure out what it was. The kitten Cupcake began climbing up Lilly's leg, determined not to be ignored during an important family talk.

"I guess it's time to face the music," Heather said.

"Did something bad happen?" Lilly asked.

"No," Heather said. "Nothing like that. This might be a very good thing. It might not happen at all.

It's just something that we've begun discussing."

"What is it?" Asked Lilly. "You're not giving very good clues right now."

Heather smiled and then said, "We've been discussing the possibility of moving to Key West, Florida. Donut Delights has an opportunity to expand there. The investor would like us to go there for at least a year. I suppose after that time, we could stay there or return to Hillside or go someplace new. There are some things that could be very exciting for us there. But it would be a change. How would you feel about it?"

Lilly thought about it. "There have been some very good things that happened for us in Hillside, but there have also been some pretty bad things too."

"She had a point," Ryan said.

"I want to support you both as much as possible. And I know Donut Delights would be successful somewhere else too because it is great," Lilly said.

Heather felt that Lilly was holding something back. "We don't need to decide this tonight," Heather said. "And if there's anything that's bothering you, we can discuss it."

"You have another year before you go to high school," Ryan said. "And I think that wherever we end up, we'd make sure that we'd stay there for your high school years. We wouldn't want to uproot you then."

Lilly smiled at her parents. She thought a bit and then said, "Okay. I think I have my answer for now."

Heather held her breath. She knew that she had been thinking about Lilly's future in the move in regards to how a successful business could provide more for her, but she realized that she did not know what Lilly's immediate feelings would be about it. If she hated the idea, would it be fair to continue considering it?

"I see how this move could be good for the family and for donut-loving people everywhere," Lilly said. "I would be willing to move on two conditions."

"A negotiation," Heather remarked.

Lilly joined her parents at the bargaining/kitchen table. Dave joined them and barked for emphasis at the importance of the moment.

"One," said Lilly. "I want to be able to video chat with my friends, Marlene and Nicolas. We could set up a computer or I could borrow your tablet for me to use. But I think we should get Nicolas a tablet too in case there's not something available at the children's shelter."

"I think we could do that," Heather said.

"It sounds doable," agreed Ryan.

"The second condition is bigger," said Lilly. "But we'd be moving because business is doing well. So, I think we'd have a little money."

"Does she want a pony?" Ryan asked.

"It's Florida," said Heather. "She must want a boat."

"I want Nicolas to be able to visit us during school breaks. If he hasn't been adopted yet, I want him to be able to stay as long as possible. And when he does get his own mom and dad, we'll just have to ask them for permission. Maybe they could visit too."

Heather and Ryan exchanged a look.

"Yes," Heather said. "We agree to these terms."

"If this move does happen, I'll make arrangements so that Nicolas can travel and stay with us. I think we've gone through enough background checks and know enough people in Hillside that it can be arranged," said Ryan.

"And we would still come back to visit," Heather assured her. "We'd have to be here for Col and Mona's wedding. And there could be other special events we come for too. We can't fly here every weekend, but I'd want to make sure to see Eva and Leila and Amy whenever we can."

"I have one more question," Lilly said.

"What?" asked Heather.

"Can we eat? Dinner smells delicious."

She laughed. Then they started eating. They enjoyed a good meal together. Dave and Cupcake were successful at begging. They might not have been as happy as if they were getting donut pieces, but they enjoyed the shrimp.

They were just deciding what they should do for their evening's activities when Ryan's phone rang. She could tell from his tone they were being called to go to a crime scene. It looked like the evening's plans were just decided for them.

Chapter 4

Heather shook her head as she arrived at the crime scene. It was the same dress boutique that she had visited with Amy and Mona earlier. However, covered with crime scene tape, Lordlittle's Lovely Gowns, looked like an entirely different place.

She was soon joined by Amy who seemed a little grumpy.

"I'm surprised you decided to tell me about this case and not just keep your plans a secret," she said.

"I know you're unhappy that I'm considering moving. But I'm just considering it. I haven't decided," Heather said. "Please don't be passive aggressive."

"I'm never passive," said Amy. "And I'm only aggressive when there's only one donut left."

Heather wasn't sure if they had completely made up, so she decided to focus on the case. "Ryan said that Sheila Lordlittle was found murdered."

"I hope this doesn't upset Mona," Amy said. Heather thought that they were going to find common ground to agree upon and move forward, but before Heather could respond, Amy added, "I think about these things because I'm one of her Maids of Honor."

"So am I," said Heather.

"I hope you're not planning on moving away from the bride in her time of need."

"I plan on catching Sheila Lordlittle's murderer," Heather said. With that, she marched up to the entrance to the boutique. Amy hurried to catch up with her.

Before either of them had a chance to air their grievances again, Ryan joined them, and they were forced to be professional.

"I have to warn you," Ryan said. "You might find this crime scene upsetting."

"Is the body still here?" Amy asked.

"No, they removed it already."

"How was she killed?" Heather asked.

"It appears to be strangulation," said Ryan.

Heather nodded. She and Amy followed Ryan towards the dressing room area. Heather was wary. Strangulation wouldn't leave much blood, so what was at the crime scene that would be so upsetting to see?

When they reached the changing area, Heather saw what he meant. The mirrors reflecting the crime scene only made it more ominous. Dresses had been ripped, and their shreds were found on the floor. The room looked like the killer had been active and angry. They had also scrawled a hateful message onto the wall: How's this for your something blue?

Heather raised a hand to her mouth in shock.

"She was strangled?" Heather asked. "So, the something blue is her corpse after she was killed?"

"The fabric that was used was also blue," Ryan said. "It looks like she was strangled with a thick piece of blue fabric. We believe it was one of the dresses, but need to examine everything."

"Either way that message is cringe-worthy," Amy said. "Why would somebody write that?"

"Why would somebody write that?" Heather asked again, considering it. "Did the killer write it before the murder to scare Ms. Lordlittle? Or after to taunt her in death?"

"Whatever way you look at it, I think we're facing a seriously scary killer," said Amy.

Heather looked around the room and at all the evidence of rage. Hopefully, there would be some DNA evidence in the room that would help point to the killer. She was about to ask when Ryan answered her question.

"The forensic team has taken many samples. Hopefully, something will provide us with a clue as to who the killer is. Unfortunately, many of these fabrics don't hold fingerprints well."

Heather looked at the writing on the wall. "Do you think we could match the handwriting here to the killer's? The G is very curly."

"It might be possible," said Ryan. "Though I think writing upright on a wall could look different than writing on a piece of paper."
"We should bring in a chalkboard and have all the suspects write on it," said Amy.

"First, we need to find our suspects," said Heather.

Chapter 5

Heather, Amy, and Ryan joined the assistant Ollie who had been waiting with an officer in the boutique office. He had been the one to find the body and call the police. However, he didn't have the look of someone who just found the dead body of someone he knew. In fact, he had a slight smile on his face when they came in.

"The customers who just happened to be in the shop today are here investigating," Ollie said. "I get it."

"We do seem to have great timing like that," Amy said. "Or

terrible timing, depending on how you look at it."

"These two are private investigators who assist the Hillside Police with certain cases," Ryan said.

Heather held back a smile. She and Amy had been helping with all the murder cases in Hillside for quite a while now. She was sure that the police (maybe excluding Hoskins) would eventually solve the crimes, but her knack for sleuthing had uncovered many important clues and caught many a killer.

"Right," Ollie said with a wink. "I get it."

"Get what?" asked Heather.

"I get what's going on here," he said.

"Would you mind enlightening us?" Ryan asked. He took out his notebook, while Amy took out a tablet. They were both ready to hear what Ollie's thoughts on this murder matter were.

"I'll play along if you want me to," Ollie said. "Do you want me to cry? Should I be angry?"

"You should be telling us what you know about this murder," Heather said.

"Right," Ollie said, winking again.

"Stop winking at my wife," Ryan said. "And tell us when you came back to the boutique."

Ollie looked uncomfortable for a moment, but then smiled and jumped into his story. "We worked until five and then closed for the day. Abigail and I left, but Ms. Lordlittle stayed behind. She does that a lot. Around seven I realized I forgot my phone charger at work. I decided to come back and see if I could get it."

"You knew that Ms. Lordlittle would still be here?" Heather asked.

"She stays late a lot," Ollie said. "So, I thought there was a good chance. And I needed to charge my phone, so if I couldn't get in and get mine, I'd have to go and buy a new one."

"Did many people know that Sheila Lordlittle was prone to working late at the shop?" Ryan asked.

Ollie shrugged. "I guess so."

"So, what happened when you arrived at the shop?" asked Ryan.

"Well, the door was unlocked, so I was able to go inside," said Ollie. "I headed towards the back to get my charger, but then I saw all the ripped fabric. So, I headed towards the changing area, and that's when I saw the performance art project."

"Performance art project?" Heather asked.

"Yeah," Ollie said. "That's what all this is, right? Mr. Lordlittle is doing something artsy. Something about the new beginnings on weddings and the endings in death? I don't always get the symbolism, but I think I understood this one."

"I think there's still a lot you don't understand," Amy said.

"Why would Sheila Lordlittle be doing performance art?" Heather asked.

"She was always going on about how she was an artist. No, an artiste. And so, she tried a new art form to attract attention," Ollie said. "And she might have thought this would be good for business. We've been a little slow, and she needed something exciting to attract customers."

"So, she killed herself in order to be an artistic business owner?" Amy asked, raising an eyebrow.

"She's not dead," Ollie said.

"Mr. Evans, Sheila Lordlittle is indeed dead," Ryan said.

"Right," Ollie said. He was about to wink again but refrained after remembering how Ryan had said to stop before.

"The medical examiner took her body away," Ryan said.

"So, nobody else could get a closer look," said Ollie.

"So we could start collecting evidence to discover who her murderer is," said Heather.

"But it's all a show," said Ollie.

"It's not," said Heather.

"You think she really was murdered?" asked Ollie.

"It would be pretty hard to strangle yourself," said Amy.

"Were there any blue dresses in your shop with special meaning?" asked Ryan.

"We had a good amount of blue dresses," said Ollie. "I guess every dress that is or is going to be part of a wedding would have special meaning. I can't think of one in particular. Blue is a popular color."

"Did you recognize the fabric on the murder weapon found on the victim?" asked Ryan.

"I remember it was blue, but I was too shocked at the time to notice anything else. I ran away to call the police. I was feeling very panicky until I realized what Ms. Lordlittle was up to," Ollie said. He paused and thought about it. "You're telling me it's really not a performance art piece?"

"I assure you it's not," said Ryan.

Ollie nodded. "Then it's to teach us a lesson."

"A customer?" asked Heather.

"No. Ms. Lordlittle. She must have been practicing, but I came back early. She probably wanted to shock Abigail and me when we came in in the morning."

"What lesson would she want to teach you?" Heather asked.

"Something about appreciating her and appreciating the one of a kind dresses. She could be a very demanding boss. She would tell us we weren't dedicated enough to the cause."

"And how did that make you feel?" asked Heather.

"Unhappy," said Ollie. "Abigail and I worked really hard sewing her crazy designs. She didn't appreciate us."

"Did you feel you needed to teach her a lesson?" asked Ryan.

Ollie looked confused and then laughed. "I get it. You're treating me like a suspect now. Like this is part of an investigation."

"This is an investigation," said Ryan. "And you are acting suspiciously."

"How did you call the police?" Heather asked, thinking of something. "If you didn't have your phone charger."

"Well, my phone wasn't dead yet," Ollie said. "It was just low battery. I was going to have to charge it that night though. I was still able to call 911."

"We can check the phone records," said Ryan.

"Guys, you're starting to freak me out. This wasn't real. Can you stop treating me like a suspect? It scares me."

"Was the door locked when you left work at five?" Heather asked.

"I don't remember," Ollie said. "I mean, I was able to leave through it."

"But you don't know if Ms. Lordlittle locked it after you?" asked Heather.

"I'm not sure," said Ollie. "I just wanted to go home."

"Was anyone with you between the time you left work and returned?" asked Ryan.

"Like an alibi?"

"Exactly like an alibi," said Ryan.

"I picked up some Chinese food so they would have seen me there, but I was home alone when I ate it. My neighbors might have seen my car though. This is intense," said Ollie. "Where are the hidden cameras?"

He looked around the room, trying to find them. He waved at

Amy's tablet, and she made a face. He was having trouble finding other spots where they could have been hidden.

"There are no hidden cameras," said Ryan.

"I know you don't want to face this," said Heather. "But Sheila Lordlittle was murdered this evening. And we need to gather all the information we can use so that we can find the murderer."

"She's really dead?" asked Ollie.

"Have you been listening to anything we said?" asked Amy.

"She was really murdered?" Ollie asked. "Somebody really did that to her?"

The knowing smile was completely gone from Ollie's face. Tears started to form in his eyes.

"I can't believe it," Ollie said. "I saw her a few hours ago. And she was so alive. I just can't believe it."

"Do you know anyone who would want to hurt her?" asked Heather.

However, now consumed with grief, Ollie wasn't paying attention to her questions. He was in his own world now. "She wasn't the best boss. But she was my boss. She could be condescending. But she also made sure the coffee maker was always working for us. I can't believe she's really, really dead."

Ollie began to cry in earnest. Heather found some tissues in her purse to give to him. She realized that they weren't going to get any more information from him that night.

Chapter 6

Heather and Ryan returned home that night with a million questions. Heather knew the answers would have to wait until the morning when they could interview more suspects and find out some of the forensic report's findings. It had been a tough night, both because of the crime and because of Amy's attitude. Heather realized that he bestie was having a strong reaction to a potential move and was going to make sure that Heather knew she was against it. They were just going to have to make sure that their little tiff didn't affect the case. Sheila Lordlittle deserved justice, and they couldn't become distracted from that.

When they entered their house, they were happily greeted. Dave and Cupcake ran to them and demanded that they be pet.

"You'd think we ignored them all night," said Eva.

Heather smiled as Eva and Leila joined them. The two older ladies were just as happy to see the Shepherds return home as the pets, but were more self-contained. Eva and Leila had started out as Heather's favorite Donut Delights customers, but were now close friends and were some of the few people she trusted to watch over Lilly on short notice.

"I know Dave and Cupcake got plenty of attention from you," Heather smiled. "They probably just think that I'm hiding donuts in my pockets."

Dave's ears perked up at the mention of donuts, but Heather just scratched him behind the ears. "False alarm, pup."

"We do have a few things to discuss though," Eva said.

"Is everything all right with Lilly?" asked Heather.

"Everything is fine," Eva assured her.

"But it is about her," said Leila.

"We miss her," said Eva. "When we were forced to be your houseguests after the fire, we got to see her all the time. And now when we babysit, we're forced to make sure she goes to sleep at her bedtime instead of hanging out with us."

"Well," Leila admitted. "Close to her bedtime."

"So, we would like you to call us over earlier to babysit so we can spend some more time with her," said Eva.

"And," Leila said. "You won't have to pay us any extra donuts in return for the extra work time."

Heather smiled. She knew the ladies were teasing her while at the same time expressing how much they missed Lilly.

"Based on this case we just took on, I have a feeling that it will allow for plenty of opportunities for you to babysit," said Heather.

"And we'll have you over for dinner again soon," offered Ryan. "We'd like to spend time with you. And I know Lilly would adore it too."

"She's like a granddaughter to us. We'd like to see her more," Eva said. "Especially…."

"Well," Leila said. "That brings us to our second discussion topic."

"Are you moving away from us?" asked Eva.

Heather and Ryan shared a look.

"We've just started thinking about it," said Heather. "Rudolph Rodney is trying to convince us to open another Donut Delights in Key West. But we haven't decided one way or another."

"Lilly was talking to us about it," said Eva. "She seems happy with the move as long as she can keep in touch with her friends."

"She told us she'd be our pen pal too," said Leila.

"There's still so much to look into," said Heather. "Besides the business aspect, we need to look into the schools there and the police force. We didn't want to tell our friends until we had a better idea of where we stood."

"Well, while you're finding your footing, you're always welcome to talk to us," said Eva.

"And we won't try to force you to walk one way or another," agreed Leila.

"But if you'd like my advice, I'd always be happy to give it," Eva said.

"I think I would like to hear it," said Heather. Eva was the woman whose advice she valued the most. She had been through so much during her long life but still remained positive and strong. Heather hoped that she would follow in her friend's footsteps as she aged.

"Do what you feel is right down deep in your gut," said Eva. "It hasn't led you astray before."

"And it has helped with your sleuthing a good deal," added Leila.

"And don't be afraid of change. You don't want to look back on things and regret a missed opportunity. Whether you stay or go, make sure it is what is best for you and your family. Don't let fear hold you back. Or, for that matter, force you to stay. Follow that gut of yours."

"Thanks, Eva."

"And one more piece of advice?"

"What?" asked Heather.

"Go get some sleep," said Eva. "I imagine you have a full day of investigating tomorrow. You'll need your rest."

***

"Thank you for coming in to speak with us," Ryan said.

"It's no trouble at all," said Abigail. "I'll help as best I can."

After Ollie's disbelief over Sheila Lordlittle's death, they had decided to use a more formal setting to talk to the other assistant. Abigail Browning had agreed to come to the police station to speak with them about her boss's death. She had not come up with various alternate ideas to dismiss the murder; she had merely asked, "Are you sure she was killed?"

"I'm afraid so," Ryan answered. "And we believe she was murdered."

"At the boutique?" Abigail asked, shuddering.

"Yes," said Heather. She and Amy were seated on either side of Ryan for the questioning, instead of next to each other. Amy was still faithfully taking notes but was letting her friend know that she was still upset.

"We're going to have to ask you some questions about when you left work to establish a time line," Heather continued. "You and Mr. Evans might have been the last people to see her alive."

"Except for the murderer, of course," Amy added.

"I left around five," Abigail said. "Ollie rushed out as soon as we closed. I wasn't in as big a hurry because I didn't have any plans that night. I said goodbye to Ms. Lordlittle and left. I didn't realize the goodbye would be so final."

"Was the door locked when you left?" Asked Heather.

"Was the door locked?" Abigail asked back.

"We'd like to establish whether it was locked or not," Heather said. "Then we can determine how the killer entered the shop."

Abigail thought about it. "It wasn't locked when I left. We never had a problem with theft before. Every dress was one of a kind so it would be easy to track down a thief. So locking up wasn't a big deal. Ms. Lordlittle normally did it herself. I don't know whether she locked it after I left or not."

Heather nodded as Amy wrote that down in her notes. She looked to Ryan. If the door was unlocked, then anyone could have come inside and killed the victim. If it was locked, then it was either someone who had a key or somebody that Sheila Lordlittle opened the door for to let inside.

"Who has copies of the store key?" Ryan asked.

"Besides Ms. Lordlittle, I think only Ollie and I have keys," said Abigail. "But we weren't supposed to be in the shop without her knowledge. It was just if we had to finish a sewing project before a wedding. Ms. Lordlittle is – was very particular."

"Was Ms. Lordlittle a difficult boss?" Heather asked.

"Very," said Abigail. "She expected absolute dedication to her, but wouldn't accept any creative input. She wanted one of a kind dresses but didn't want any new ideas. That was very frustrating. She thought of Ollie and me as sewing machines, not as future designers."

"Did that upset you?" asked Ryan.

"I know you want to ask me about it, so just ask," said Abigail. "I know you spoke to Ollie. He must have told you about our fight."

"What fight?" asked Heather.

"He didn't say anything?" Abigail asked. "I was sure when you started asking questions about who had a problem with her that he would have mentioned it."

"Ollie was preoccupied," Amy said. "He had trouble accepting the death."

"What was the fight about?" asked Heather.

"It was two days ago," Abigail said. "And it was about what I was just telling you. About how she didn't want us to contribute to any designs. She wouldn't let us make our own designs for the store either. I was really mad at the time. I told her that all her recent designs looked ridiculous. I think that's why she was really pushing them when you visited with your friend who is getting married. She wanted to show me that she could sell one of them."

"Fat chance," Amy said. "Not that I want to speak ill of the dead."

"There was still some tension between us, but I hoped eventually she would come around," said Abigail. "I designed some dresses that I think brides would love."

"Where were you after work?" Heather asked.

"I wish I had a better alibi," Abigail said. "I didn't have any real plans. I was home alone. I just ate dinner and watched a movie. I bought the movie on demand though. Maybe you could check that? You could see that I watched it."

"We could check it," Ryan said. "But that would only prove that you played the movie. It doesn't prove that you stayed to watch the whole thing."

"I could answer questions about it," said Abigail. "To prove I watched it."

"No spoilers," piped up Amy.

"Thank you for the offer, Miss Browning," said Ryan. "I think we have some other questions to ask you instead."

"I have a question too," said Abigail. "That is if it's all right."

Ryan nodded, inviting her to proceed. Sometimes a question that a suspect or a witness asked could be as telling as the answers that they gave.

"Ms. Lordlittle's death, well," Abigail began. "I heard it was somewhat brutal. Was the killer just going after a woman who was alone? Or was he going after Mr. Lordlittle? If I was there, would I have been killed too? Or could I have saved her?"

"That's more than one question," Amy said, trying to lighten tension with a joke.

"We can't tell how a killer would have reacted under different circumstances," Ryan said. "But we do believe that Ms. Lordlittle was targeted in particular."

"We could read the handwriting on the wall," said Amy.

"I see," said Abigail.

"Do you know anyone who would want to harm Ms. Lordlittle?" Heather asked. "Maybe an unhappy customer?"

"We had a few of those," Abigail said. "There was only one who we called the police on."

Ryan nodded and looked to Heather. "Based on that information that you gave me before about that, I asked Hoskins to find the police report on it." He turned back to Abigail, "But, Miss Browning, why don't you tell us what you remember about the incident?"

"It was about a week ago. I was sewing in the back room when I heard shouting, and I came out to see a bride screaming at Ms. Lordlittle. She probably would have hit her if her maid of honor wasn't holding her back. Ollie and I called the police, and they asked the bride to leave. She threatened Ms. Lordlittle on her way out."

"What did she say?" Asked Heather.

"Something like "you can't get away with what you did, and you'll be sorry." Then the policeman and her maid of honor got her to walk away," said Abigail.

"What had made her so angry?" asked Ryan.

"She said that her wedding dress was basically see-through. But Ms. Lordlittle said it was part of the design," said Abigail. "Ms. Lordlittle didn't seem especially phased by the bride's concerns, and I think that's what set her off. She wanted a reaction from Ms. Lordlittle."

"Was there anyone else who wanted to harm your employer?" Heather asked. She knew they could find out more information about this angry bride from the police report, but wanted to know more about other suspects that they should consider.

"We've had a few angry customers. I wouldn't have thought that it would escalate to murder except that now she is dead," said Abigail.
"Could you write those names down for us?" Heather asked.

Ryan provided Abigail with a pencil and paper, and she began writing.

"I'm sorry I don't know everyone's name. But you could trace who they are by the dress description. Ms. Lordlittle kept great notes," said Abigail.

Heather examined the list as it was slid over to her: bride and maid of honor from police call, mermaid blue dress, teal corset dress. They would have to examine the records to determine who the people were. She doubted anyone would ever be named "Mermaid Blue."

"Thank you for answering our questions," Ryan said. "Before you leave an officer is going to show you some pieces of fabric to see if you can identify what any of them came from."

"Of course," said Abigail. Ryan showed her to another room. Heather looked to Amy.

"I think our suspect list just grew," she said.

Chapter 7

Heather brought out some Chocolate Chocolate Donuts for her team to enjoy. She could already tell that this was going to be a difficult case. They needed some chocolate to keep their spirits up.

Hoskins heard the sound of a donut box opening and hurried over to where they were at the police station.

"Hi partner," he said. "I found that police report you wanted."

He grabbed one of the Chocolate Chocolate Donuts before handing over the report. Heather was reminded of her discussion with Ryan about the chocolate fingerprints on evidence and hoped they weren't about to see a repeat of the behavior. Ryan intercepted the report and started looking through it.

"Thanks," Hoskins said as bit into a donut. "I could use some more energy. These should give me a boost."

"You need more energy because of how hard you've been working on this case?" Amy asked.

"I did track down that report," Hoskins said with slight indignation. "But that's not why I'm tired. I wasn't at the crime scene last night because I was meeting with the mayor. He wanted to shake my hand."

Heather and Amy exchanged a look. They were thinking the same thing and both hoping that Hoskins had washed any sticky candy residue off of it first.

"That must have been very exciting for you," Ryan said.

"Yes and no," said Hoskins. "I happy that someone important wanted to talk to me and recognize how good I am at what I do."

"What you do?" Amy asked. Heather nudged her in the ribs.

They shouldn't outright insult Ryan's partner. He was trying to be nicer to them too. He at least thanked her for the donuts today.

"But it was tiring too. I thought he was just going to shake my hand and then we'd eat dinner."

"You ate dinner with the mayor?" Heather asked.

"Yeah. The mayor and his wife, and me and my wife, and the woman I helped on our last case Crystal Rahway. We had this great meal. And I really wanted to focus on the food. But he kept bringing the topic of conversation back to the police force. He wanted to know where we needed upgrades and help and stuff."

"The mayor wants to provide us more support?" Ryan asked. "That's wonderful."

"Yeah," Hoskins said. "He kept asking for specific things to help with."

"Did you tell him about how some of the police car radios aren't clear? Or how the computers in the bullpen could be updated? Or did you ask for some exciting riot gear equipment, just in case?" Ryan asked with a smile.

"Oh," Hoskins said. "I told him that the break room could use a cappuccino machine and maybe one of those fancy vending machines that have sandwiches."

The smile was gone from Ryan's face. "I see," he said. "I think we should probably focus on this case now."

"Sure," Hoskins said. "Do you think one of those ladies from the report is the killer?"

"They certainly could be," Heather said. "If they were angry enough about a wedding dress to fight in the store, they might have been angry enough to come back and kill the victim."

"And the something blue threat that was written on the wall was about their wedding," Amy said. "She felt blue because of the dress?"

"Speaking of blue," Heather said. "Could we see the fabric that was found at the crime scene?"

"Sure," Ryan said. "And Abigail might have identified some of it by now."

Heather was not surprised to see that Hoskins decided to wait by the donut box and "work on his own lead" while they went to look at the fabric remains.

The pieces of fabric had all been bagged and labeled but were spread out on a table. An officer smiled at Ryan and handed him Abigail's statement about the fabric. Then he left them to make their own examination.

"It looks as if Abigail Browning believes that all the scraps that were found at the crime scene came from dresses that were still in their store. She wasn't one hundred percent on all of them. But she gave the names of some of them. She's fairly certain they were all currently on sale in the shop," Ryan said.

"I believe it," Amy said. "Those orange pieces look like the first bridesmaid dress that Heather tried on."

Ryan couldn't resist a chuckle. "This is what Mona considered to have you in at her wedding?"

"Believe me, it didn't look much better before it was torn up," said Amy.

"She's not joking," Heather agreed.

"Some of these other pieces of material look familiar too," Amy said. "We might have seen them in the shop."

Heather looked at the pieces. They were all about a foot wide in their tears, and it looked as if at least a dozen dresses were destroyed.

"The killer must have been furious to inflict all this damage on the dresses and then on the victim," Heather said.

"Do you think it was a Bridezilla that went on the attack?" Amy asked.

"It very well could be," said Heather. "But what about the murder weapon?"

"That piece of fabric Abigail Browning wasn't able to identify," Ryan said.

"Is that because it was part of a dress that had already been out of the shop for a while? Something that she hadn't sold?" Heather asked.

"Or was it just too small a sample to identify?" Amy asked.

Ryan showed them the evidence bag that held the cloth that had served as the murder weapon to strangle Sheila Lordlittle. It was a thick blue fabric that was about three feet long.

"It looks like this was part of a dress too," Heather said.

"I think so too," said Amy. "The fold there makes it looks like it's part of the skirt."

"So, the question is," Heather said. "Was this dress used to kill the victim because it was easily accessible? Or because it was the reason the killer wanted to kill?"

Chapter 8

"Should we be scared about approaching her?" Amy asked. "What if Bridezilla morphs into Wifezilla? What if she attacks us?"

"She won't attack us with Ryan here with us," Heather assured her.

Ryan made the motion of tipping his hat to reassure them, and they smiled. The three of them walked up to the door of the suspect's house.

"And besides," Heather said as she knocked on the door. "We've faced worse before."

"Not reassuring," said Amy.

The door opened, and a woman with blond hair opened the door.

"Tabitha Greenwald?" Ryan asked.

"Yes," she said. "It's a new last name, so it still sounds a little funny to my ears, but that's me. Who are you?"

"I'm Detective Ryan Shepherd with the Hillside Police," he said, showing his badge. "This is Heather Shepherd and Amy Givens, who are licensed investigators who assist on certain cases."

"What's going on? Did something happen to Harold?" she asked.

"No, ma'am," Ryan said. "We're here about Sheila Lordlittle."

Tabitha Greenwald groaned. "I'm never going to live that down. I did lose my cool. But she deserved a good yelling at. I wanted to hit her, but Holly held me back."

"Holly was the maid of honor who was at the store with you?" Heather doubled checked.

"Yes," said Tabitha. "Now what is this about? Is she trying to press charges? Some sort of verbal assault thing? Fine. I was going to contact a lawyer anyway to sue that trickster."

"Did Ms. Lordlittle know about this lawsuit?" Ryan asked.

"Not yet," said Tabitha. "But she will. Especially if she has cops coming to my house to get me in trouble for yelling."

"We're not here about that incident at the shop," said Ryan. "We're investigating her murder."

"Her murder?" Tabitha asked.

"Yes," Ryan said. "And you admitted that you had an issue with the victim?"

"I did," Tabitha said. "But I didn't kill her. I didn't even know she was dead. It would have been pretty stupid of me to admit all that to the police if I killed her."

"Yeah, it would," said Amy. They all looked at her. "Well, it would."

"Please, come inside," Tabitha said, showing the way.

Tabitha led them into the living room where there enough seats for them all to sit. The home was still filled with boxes of wedding gifts. Some were unwrapped and others were not. The coffee table in the living room had a coffee table book that had never been opened. There were some pictures on the wall from her wedding, but they were all cropped to only show the faces. Every picture was from the neck up.

"We saw the police report, but why don't you tell us about when you visited her shop yourself?" Heather said.

"To understand what I said in the shop, you have to understand what she did to me. She ruined my wedding," Tabitha said.

"She really ruined your wedding?" Amy asked. "You're not being dramatic?"

"I tried on her dress in her shop and it looked lovely, though a little sheer. I told her my wedding was going to be an outdoor wedding, and she said it would be fine. Still, I asked her to adjust the sheerness a bit. She finished at the last minute so I could only make sure it still fit the night before my wedding. Well, the day of the wedding, outside in the bright sun, I discovered that she made the dress even sheerer. You could practically see through it! It was like I was naked in front of my whole family and my groom's family."

"That's like the nightmare of being naked in front of your classroom," Amy said.

"Real life is much worse," Tabitha assured her.

"And you blamed Sheila Lordlittle for this?" Heather asked.

"Of course," Tabitha said. "She changed the dress and turned it into something scandalous. Then when I confronted her in the shop after I came back from my honeymoon, she showed no remorse. She said it was part of the design, and she couldn't help it if I didn't have the body to pull it off."

"Rude," Amy said. "And not accurate. I bet you were a beautiful bride. Even if everyone saw a little too much of you."

"Thank you," Tabitha said. "Holly really was my saving grace. As soon as the ceremony was over and she realized the problem, she went into action. She found a nice coat for me to throw over my dress. It looked like it was an intentional style. Maybe some people were able to believe that what they saw was a trick of the light. I destroyed most of the photos."

"And confronting Ms. Lordlittle did nothing to ease this pain?" Heather asked.

"No," Tabitha said. "She was completely unimpressed by my valid complaints. It made me so mad."

"And did you visit her again?" Heather asked.

"No," Tabitha said. "Holly convinced me that talking to her wouldn't get my money back. I'd have to seek alternate routes if I wanted justice."

"What sort of alternate route?" asked Heather.

"Not murder," Tabitha said. "Legal action to get a refund. Or bad press to hurt her business. I'm sure I'm not the only one who had issues with her."

"No, but you were the only one that the police had to be called on," said Heather. "Which is why we needed to speak with you."

"Where were you last evening between five thirty and seven p.m.?" Ryan asked.

"Well," Tabitha said. "My husband and I were returning some wedding gifts last evening. We must have still been in the store at that time. We ended up getting three toaster ovens."

"We'll look into that," Ryan said.

"I told you I didn't kill her," Tabitha Greenwald said.

"One more question," Heather said. "What color were your bridesmaid dresses?"

"They were maroon," Tabitha said, bitterly. "And not see through."

Chapter 9

Ryan had to go and talk to the medical examiner to see if there were any new findings, and then check in with his partner, so Amy and Heather were left alone together.

"What do you make of her?" Heather asked.

"If she's telling the truth about her alibi, then she couldn't have strangled her even if she wanted to," Amy said.

"That's true," said Heather. "She does have a motive, but I'm not sure she did it."

"She had maroon bridesmaid dresses too," said Amy. "The murder weapon couldn't have come from her."

"It still might have been something that was found in the shop," said Heather. "And Abigail just didn't remember it."

"Do you think either of the assistants did it?" Amy asked.

"Their motives don't seem as strong as having your wedding ruined, but neither of the assistants have strong alibis," said Heather. "However, this case is definitely making me appreciate my assistants at Donut Delights."

"They'd cry worse than Ollie if you left them," Amy said. "They'd be devastated. Whether you were murdered. Or, you know, you chose to pack up and leave them."

"I never said I was moving," Heather said.

"You never said you weren't moving," Amy pointed out.

Heather didn't know what to say to that, so she just said, "Come on."

"Where are we going?"

"We have another suspect to interview," Heather said. "I think we should meet Holly."

"The Maid of Honor?"

"Tabitha Greenwald made it sound as if her maid of honor would do anything for her."

"Does that include murder?" Amy asked.

"I think we should find out," said Heather.

***

"I don't understand why you're talking to me," Holly Lag said. "I was the reasonable one in all this."

Heather had already introduced herself and Amy as private

investigators and Holly was debating whether to let them inside her house or not.

"Miss Lag," Heather said. "We're just trying to uncover the truth about a murder. If you and Tabitha Greenwald had nothing to do with it, then we should be out of your way shortly. The sooner we dismiss you as suspects, the sooner we can move on."

Holly opened the door and allowed them inside.

"I don't like to speak ill of the dead," Holly said. "But Lordlittle was in the wrong about the dress. She shouldn't have done what she did to Tabitha's dress. And she should have offered her a refund when we went to talk to her."

"Tabitha said that when the talk didn't go well with Ms. Lordlittle, you said that you would have to seek alternate means to find justice," Heather started.

"I meant finding a lawyer," said Holly. "She turned a beautiful wedding dress into something sleazy. She embarrassed my best friend on what should have been the happiest day of her life. I thought we should sue her."

"Are you sure you didn't want a more permanent form of justice?" asked Heather.

"I didn't kill her," said Holly.

"Just because she was looking out for her friend's interests, doesn't mean she's a murderer," Amy said.

"Thank you," Holly said.

"That's what Maids of Honor do," said Amy.

"Exactly," Holly said.

"They help their friends when they have a dress malfunction," Amy said.

"Yes."

"They don't move away from them while they're still planning their wedding and still have a million things to do to get ready for it," Amy continued. Holly wasn't sure if she should agree to that though.

"Miss Lag, where were you last evening?" Heather asked, deciding to focus on the case instead of personal squabbles.

"I was home alone," Holly sighed. "I'm not married yet. But I did catch the bouquet."

"The bouquet? That's wonderful," said Amy. "Picking out a bouquet is an important part of wedding planning. Maids of honor help with those decisions too."

"I did," said Holly.

"And then you were rewarded with catching it," said Amy. "That's great. I'm glad you were such a dedicated bridesmaid. It's an honor to be chosen as one, and sometimes people forget that."

"I never forgot that," said Holly. "I did everything I could to help Tabitha's day go smoothly. But the dress did get in the way of a perfect day."

"Miss Lag, does the phrase "How's this for your something blue?" mean anything to you?" Heather asked.

"Does it refer to the "something old, something new, something borrowed, something blue" poem for weddings?" Holly asked. "That's all I can think of. We got Tabitha this cute little blue garter for her something blue. Unfortunately, more people saw it than we wanted."

"But remembering to fulfill that rhyme is important Maid of Honor work," said Amy. "And you were on top of everything."

"I really tried to be," said Holly.

128

"You weren't about to abandon the bride in her time of need," Amy continued.

"No, of course not," said Holly. "If we had gotten the dress any earlier than I could have fixed that too."

"But Ms. Lordlittle made everything difficult and ruined things for you," said Amy.

"She really did."

"And you would do anything for the bride?" asked Amy.

"Of course," said Holly.

"Even seek revenge for her?"

Holly realized what she had verbally walked into. "I draw the line at murder," she said.

Chapter 10

"That was a smart idea," Heather said. "You got Holly to admit that she would do practically anything for her friend the bride."

"I know. I'm amazing," said Amy.

"It was a good tactic," said Heather. "I thought you were really angry with me. But you were getting suspect to talk."

"Well, you know, one stone, two birds. That sort of thing," said Amy.

They got into the car and drove in silence. Heather realized she was going to have to make a decision about her move soon. She was either going to have to reassure her bestie that she wasn't going anywhere, or she was going to have to give details about her move and tell her friend to deal with it. This "in between" was causing them both stress.

After Heather had dropped Amy off at her house, she decided to drive over to Owen's Tea Shop. After hearing so much about Maid of Honor duties, she should check in to see how Mona was holding up after the murder at the dress shop. Heather realized she might also have an opportunity to talk to Col about the potential business deal.

"Heather," Col said, smiling when he saw her. "I've found the perfect tea to complement your Chocolate Chocolate Donut."

Heather moved closer and allowed him to pour her a cup of a chocolate infused tea. She wasn't always a fan of tea, but she found the flavors that Col prepared to be light and delicious. She felt guilty about cheating on her favorite drink coffee, but couldn't help enjoying the drinks that Col brewed, especially when they were paired with some Donut Delights dishes.

"This is wonderful," Heather said. "I wish I had some more donuts to have with it, but I've been running around questioning suspects all morning."

"No need to worry," Col said. "Mona brought some in for us. She really likes this new flavor. But what's not to like?"

Heather smiled, and they both sat down at a table to chat.

"Is Mona here?" Heather asked.

"She is," Col said with a note of worry in his voice. "But she's not quite herself today. She wasn't feeling too well. She's resting in the employee room right now. You're welcome to go back and see her, but first, I have a few questions to ask."

"Business or wedding?" Heather asked.

"Business," said Col, "Mona told me that a man was trying to get you to move to Florida and open up another store. Is this a crazy man? Or is this something you want to consider?"

"It's something I want to consider, but I haven't had much of a chance to do so yet," said Heather. "I need to find out more details. And I wanted to talk to you about it too."

"No need to be nervous," Col said. "I didn't think this move was about you running out on our current business arrangement."

"Working with you has helped my online orders to grow," said Heather.

"I know," Col said. "It's been exciting. Those donuts have been traveling all around the country."

"And it's become so busy that it is hard to keep up with them. Another location might be a good idea."

"And this man is offering a location in Florida?"

"His name is Rudolph Rodney," said Heather. "He's Roadkill Rodney's uncle. He has some property on Duval Street, and would like me to set up a second Donut Delights there."

"It does seem like a good opportunity," Col said.

"You're not against it?" Heather asked.

"Of course not," Col said. "We're partners. What's good for Donut Delights is good for Owen's Tea Shop. But I would want to make sure that this is a good business deal for you. I'm sure Ryan could do a thorough background check on him. And would you mind if I spoke to him at some point before you make an official decision?"

"Not at all," Heather said with a smile.

She was feeling in good spirits when she went in search of Mona, but as soon as she found her, the happy mood was lost. Heather was immediately worried for her friend. She looked like she hadn't slept at all and a sense of sadness pervaded from her.

"Mona, what's wrong?" Heather asked.

Heather sat down next to her and held her hands. Mona looked like she was about to cry.

"Heather, I'm glad you're here," said Mona. "I could use a friend."

"I'm always here for you," Heather said.

"I think I have to call off the wedding."

"Why?" asked Heather. "Did Col do something?"

"No," said Mona.

"And do you still love him?"

"Of course I do," Mona said. "How can you ask that?"

"Then why do you have to call off the wedding?" Heather asked.

"Isn't it obvious?" Mona said. "Our wedding is cursed. This is the second time that someone has been murdered while I was planning my wedding. It's not meant to be."

"Mona, those crimes didn't have anything to do with you," Heather assured her. "We were just near the wrong place at the wrong time."

"Exactly," said Mona. "The universe is trying to tell me that Col and I aren't supposed to get married. How many people have to die until I get the message?"
"I don't believe that for a moment," Heather said. "You and Col are meant to be together."

"Maybe to be together, but not married," Mona said. "Let's face it. Marriages don't seem to work out for me."

"Your last marriage didn't work out," Heather admitted. "But that doesn't mean you don't deserve love. If you and Col love each other and want to become husband and wife, then that should be the only thing that matters."

"Do you really think so?" Mona asked.

"Things weren't always easy for Ryan and me," Heather said. "And if we let a murder get in our way, we never would have started dating, let alone get married."

Mona laughed. "It's different for you two. You're super sleuths."

"I'll take the compliment," Heather said.

"Do you really think Col and I belong together?" Mona asked.

"I do," said Heather. "But the important question is whether you believe it."

"I love him more than anything," said Mona. "I love working with him. I love being with him. I do want to marry him, but I don't want him to inherit my bad luck that I seem to have with nuptials."

"Would you be willing to inherit his bad luck if it were the other way around?"

"I would," Mona said. She thought about it. "Thank you so much, Heather. You're right. If we want to get married, then we should."

"I'm glad I could help."

"My feet aren't cold anymore," Mona said. "Thanks for being my slippers."

She gave her a hug.

"I'll miss you if you leave," Mona said.

Chapter 11

Heather was walking with Dave and Cupcake, or rather, she was standing with Dave and Cupcake as they smelled a patch of mud for what seemed like an incredibly long time. Fulfilling her promise to Eva and Leila that they could spend more time with Lilly, the two acting grandmothers were playing a card game with Lilly and Nicolas. Heather would be happy to join them soon but needed a moment of quiet to clear her mind. She was happy that the animals needed another walk so she could enjoy some time thinking. However, she was even happier when she saw Ryan walking towards her to join her.

"What's so interesting about that mud?" he asked.

"I have no idea," Heather said. "Maybe you could tell me."

"It just looks like mud to me. Maybe it smells interesting, but I'll leave it up to Dave to figure that out."

Heather gave her husband a kiss. "I'm glad you got out of work in time to join me."

He took one of the leashes. "Me too," he said.

"Anything new about the case?" Heather asked.

"The medical examiner confirmed what we already thought about the cause of death as strangulation and the time of death between five thirty and seven," Ryan said. "And Hoskins continues to get praise for doing nothing."

"I don't understand how the chief can play along with this."

"Me neither," said Ryan.

"Well, the best thing we can do is solve this current case," said Heather. "Maybe then they'll remember who the real detective in town is."

"You?' Ryan joked.

"You're the real detective," Heather said. "But Amy and I are the real P.I.s. She's still mad at me though."

"I hope it's not affecting your ability to work the case together," Ryan said, echoing a worry of hers.

"I don't think so," said Heather. "But it's starting to hurt my feelings. If Amy were going to move, I'd be sad and disappointed, but I don't think I'd make her feel bad about it."

"Maybe this is just Amy's sense of humor," Ryan suggested. "It can be a little off sometimes."

"Maybe," Heather said without really believing it. She knew that Amy was upset about the potential move and was trying to sabotage the idea in her head.

"Do you have any thoughts on the case?"

"Lots of thoughts, but no new evidence," said Heather. "No one has a good alibi, except the unhappy bride who had the best motive. So far, I'm not sure if anyone of the remaining suspects had enough anger to not only strangle the victim but to destroy the dresses in the store and to write on the wall."

"There are some more unhappy customers to speak to," said Ryan. "Maybe one of them is the killer."

"Maybe," said Heather. "Did I tell you that I saw Col and Mona today?"

"How is she holding up after the murder?" Ryan asked.

"She wasn't doing too well at first," Heather admitted. "She started thinking that she and Col weren't meant to be together."

"That's ridiculous," said Ryan.

"That's what I told her. And she seems better now," said Heather.

"Then you were a great Maid of Honor."

"Tell that to Amy," Heather grumbled.

"She'll come around," Ryan said.

Dave and Cupcake finally became bored with their sniffing, and they began walking again. In fact, they began picking up the pace to make up for lost time, and the humans had to hurry after them.

"Col has come around," Heather said. "He thinks the move might be good for business, but he wants to talk to Rudolph Rodney before we make our decision."

"I'd like to do that too," said Ryan.

"I think we should arrange a meeting," Heather said. "Let's get all the information, and then make our decision."

"Agreed," Ryan said.

Then they had to run with the pets, who just as suddenly became tired and started sniffing a new patch of mud.

A thought entered Heather's head. "Mona was upset because two murders happened when she was planning her wedding."

"Right," Ryan said. "But you convinced her it wasn't her fault.

There has been a decent amount of crime in Hillside recently."

"But remember who the killer was last time when it was related to picking flowers?" Heather asked. "It was related to Lyle Clarke."

"I know that evil mob tied contractor has been involved in several murders," Ryan said. "But I don't see what he could gain this time. I don't think the land that the boutique is on is valuable."

"Promise you'll look into it," Heather said. "I'd hate to leave Hillside knowing that he's still around and causing menace."

"I promise. And I'd like to see him behind bars too," said Ryan. "But I really don't think he's involved in this case. This crime seems more personal. Both with the cause of death and with the way the scene was found."

"I guess you're right," Heather said. "Most likely it was a bride."

"And you have some more interviews to conduct with unhappy bridal customers?"

"I do."

Chapter 12

"Betsy Gene?" Heather asked as "Blue Mermaid Dress" opened her door.

"Yes," Betsy said. She was a small woman with dark hair and freckles. She also looked puzzled to find the two women standing on her porch.

"I'm Heather Shepherd, and this is Amy Givens. We're private investigators consulting on a case with the Hillside Police. Do you mind if we ask you some questions?"

"Not at all," said Betsy. "But what is this about? Is it about the grocery store down the street? I thought they were serving outdated food."

"No," Heather started.

"Is it about the car accident near by job the other day? I was making a coffee run, so I didn't see anything."

"No," Heather started again.

"Is it about my neighbor Mrs. Puttman? She's a hoarder, isn't she? She's not hoarding anything dangerous, is she?"

"Miss Gene, we're here about Sheila Lordlittle," said Heather.

"The dress lady?" Betsy asked. "Why? Is there a class action lawsuit against her? I'd join. My dress was terrible."

"And you were angry about this dress?" Heather asked.

"It made me look like a pregnant fish," Betsy said.

"I don't see how that could be," Amy said. "How?"

Betsy invited them inside and then found a picture from her sister's wedding.

"Yeah," Amy said. "Actually, that's exactly how I would describe it. A pregnant fish."

"Why did you buy the dress if you were so unhappy with it?" Heather asked.

"My sister was getting married in Austin," Betsy said. "She chose the color of fabric for her bridesmaid but said that we could choose the style of the dress so it would look nice on all our different body types. But because we were all going to have different dresses, she encouraged us to make sure that every dress was different. It would look silly if two people had the same and three were different."

"Right," Amu agreed.

"So, I went to the dress shop that said it had one of a kind dresses and asked if they would make one with this fabric. Sheila Lordlittle agreed, but she finished it right before the wedding. I didn't have time to get anything else made with the fabric, so I wore that dress. Well, my sister certainly didn't have any bridesmaids that had the same dress like me."

"Were you angry about this?" Heather asked. "An employee remembered you being upset in the shop."

"I was upset when I picked it up," Betsy said. "I didn't want to look stupid at my sister's wedding. I think I yelled and then cried. But there was nothing else I could do. I needed to wear a dress from that fabric, so I angrily paid for it and left."

"Did you ever return to the boutique?" Heather asked.

"No," Betsy said. "I avoided it for sure."

"You didn't go there two nights ago?" asked Heather.

"No," Betsy said. "What did you say you were investigating again?"

"Sheila Lordlittle was murdered," Heather said.

"I didn't have anything to do with that," Betsy said. "I was mad at the time. Maybe even still a little mad. But I do realize that I have a funny story because of this. I wasn't going to kill anyone over this."

"Your bridesmaid dress was blue," Heather commented.

"Yes," Betsy said. "My sister wanted all her bridesmaids to be her something blue. You know, according to the saying."

Heather and Amy exchanged a look. Then they looked at the picture of the bridesmaid dress again. It was hard to see the exact coloring based on the lighting. It might have been the same shade as the murder weapon.

"Do you still have this dress?" Heather asked.

"We'd love to see it," Amy said. "Both professionally and for fun."

"I got rid of it as soon as the wedding was over," Betsy said. "I wanted to burn it, but was less dramatic and just threw it in the trash."

"So, you no longer have the dress or any of its fabric?" Heather clarified.

"Right," Betsy said.

"Were any of the other bridesmaids from Hillside?" Amy asked.

"No," said Betsy. "It was my sister's friends from Austin, me and our cousin from Virginia."

"Was your sister angry about the dress?" Heather asked.

"She thought it was hysterical. It was probably the best wedding present I could have given."

"Do you happen to know where your sister was two days ago?" asked Heather.

"She's on a trip to Europe," Betsy said. "Do you think she's a suspect?"

"We need to rule out all possibilities," Heather said.

"Well, I'm not a possibility," Betsy said. "I didn't kill anybody. Rule me out too."

"Where were you two nights ago?"

"I went to bingo," said Betsy. "It takes up most of the evening."

"We'll check on that," Heather said. "Thank you for your time. We'll be in touch if we have any more questions."

Heather and Amy walked away from the house and wondered about the woman they had just questioned.

"I could understand her getting rid of the ugly dress," Heather said.

"After seeing, yes, defininitely," agreed Amy.

"But she might have kept it to use to kill Sheila Lordlittle and then lied about when she got rid of it."

"The dress was blue and might match the killer shade," said Amy.

"She also mentioned the something blue saying," Heather commented.

"Something definitely smells fishy," said Amy.

Chapter 13

June Grady was much quieter than any of the other suspects that she had questioned. She had admitted the private investigators without a fuss and waited for their questions.

"Thank you for speaking with us," Heather said.

Amy echoed the sentiments and took out the tablet to take notes.

"This is about Sheila Lordlittle?" June asked.

"Yes," Heather admitted. "We're assisting the police in investigating her murder."

"I'm not sure what I can tell you," June said. "But I'll try my best."

"How well did you know Ms. Lordlittle?" Heather asked.

"Not that well," said June. "I bought my wedding dress there. I spent more than I should have. Even more obviously now."

"What do you mean by that?" asked Heather.

"I suppose I should just say it," June said. "It's difficult for me to admit it. I don't like having to say it out loud. They say it will get easier in time."

"What are you confessing to?" Amy asked. "Is it the murder? Is our job that easy?"

"I didn't kill anyone," June said. "Then what are you talking about?"

"I made all these wedding preparations, but I never got married," June said. "I was left at the altar."

"That's terrible," Amy said.

"Was is Ms. Lordlittle's fault?" Heather asked.

"We heard she ruined some other weddings," Amy said.

"No," June said. "It was all my fault. I drove my groom away."

"How?" Heather asked, hoping to get her talking and that it might lead to clues in the case.

"As soon as I got that ring on my finger, I really did become another person. I became obsessed with my wedding. I wanted everything to be perfect. But I started to forget about people and feelings. I became crazy. I fought with Sheila Lordlittle about the dress, even though it was beautiful and was what I bought. Because I was a bride, I felt I was entitled to more. I made my bridesmaids cry. In the end, I told my fiancé that I didn't want his brother in the wedding party because of a haircut he got. It wasn't even that bad of a haircut. My fiancé said he didn't recognize me anymore. I was about to get nitpicky when we made our vows, and he realized it. He left me instead of saying his."

"Wow," Amy said. "That's terrible."

"The terrible thing is that I know it was my fault," said June. "I should have been trying to make our two families come together and not make my groom choose between his family and me. Especially for a stupid reason."

"But Ms. Lordlittle had nothing to do with the issues at your wedding?" Heather asked.

"No. Just my own obsession," she said. "I was supposed to be a June bride."

Amy refrained from making a comment.

"But you did say you fought with her at the boutique?" asked Heather.

"I was making unreasonable demands," June said. "I kept coming in for fittings and adjustments. The staff learned to fear when June Grady was entering the shop. I think they called me a "Grady A Nightmare" behind my back. I probably was."

"There's no ill feelings towards them now?"

"No," June said. "I realize now that the flaws were all mine. I need to focus on myself now to see who I want to be. Maybe then I can talk to my former fiancé again, or I can look for love somewhere new."

"That seems very big of you," Heather said. "I do have to ask where you were two night ago."

"I was with a friend," June said. "Actually, she was one of my bridesmaids. The one I didn't scare away. We had dinner and drinks."

"What color were your bridesmaid dresses?" Amy asked.

"They were teal," June said. "And probably not very comfortable. I think I have a picture."

June searched and found a picture of her friend modeling the dress. She also gave Heather her friend's name and contact information to confirm her alibi. However, Heather and Amy were more focused on the dress. The color wasn't quite right, but it had a sash on it in the same shape as the fabric used to strangle Sheila Lordlittle.

Chapter 14

Heather returned home with thoughts of the dresses swirling around her mind. There were ruined dresses at the crime scene that seemed to have been destroyed in anger. There was part of a dress that was used to kill the victim. Was what was used to kill Sheila Lordlittle from Betsy Gene's dress that she claimed to have gotten rid of? Was it part of a sash like on June Grady's bridesmaid dresses? Was it from a dress that was in the boutique? Or was it in someone's possession before the killing?

"You look lost in thought," Ryan said.

"Yes," Heather said. "I'm thinking about the case and feeling lost."

"I do have some good news," said Ryan.

"They found DNA at the crime scene after all?"

"No. Nothing like a slam dunk for the case. But I picked up a pizza on my way home, and Eva and Leila are going to join us for dinner."

Heather suddenly realized that she was ravenous. The smell of the pizza made her mouth water, and she knew how well her Chocolate Chocolate Donuts would go with it for dessert.

"You're the best," she said.

The smell of the pizza must have reached Dave's nose too because he wandered into the room, looking for a snack. Heather wasn't going to open the food until their guests arrived, so she made Dave be content with some tummy petting.

"I did look into the Lyle Clarke angle today," Ryan said.

"And?"

"And nothing," he said. "There doesn't appear to be any connection at all to Lordlittle's Lovely Gown and him. His businesses aren't interested in the land, and I don't believe he ever crossed paths with Sheila Lordlittle."

"It was worth a try," Heather said. "He's involved in so many crimes in Hillside; it made sense to check whether he was involved with this."

"How were your interviews?"

"The other unhappy customers seem to have alibis. It's possible that Betsy Gene's blue bridesmaid dress was where the murder weapon came from, but it's impossible to tell for sure. We're matching the color based on a photo, and she claims to have gotten rid of it long ago," Heather said. "Forensics hasn't discovered anything new with their tests?"

"Unfortunately not," said Ryan. "The fabric didn't hold much. This was a shop, so there was evidence from people that were there before, but nothing is a match for anything in the system. We found some hair that matches Ollie Evans and Abigail Browning at the crime scene, but that could have been there from before the murder because they worked there."

"True," Heather said. "We saw them in the changing rooms when we were there ourselves."

"That's all our something old for the case," Ryan said.

"I'd like something new," Heather said. "Like the solution."

Ryan chuckled.

"I feel like I'm missing something with the fabric," Heather said.

"The murder weapon or the dresses that were turned into one-foot shreds?" Ryan asked.

"Both," she responded. "Could I look at them again tomorrow?"

"Of course," Ryan said. "Do you know what's bothering you about them?"

Before she could answer, they heard a knocking at the door. They opened it and greeted Eva and Leila. Lilly came over to meet them at the door too, fresh from working on a new story on her pink typewriter.

"We're so happy to see you all," Eva said.

"And to have some pizza and donuts," said Leila.

They started towards the table and passed out the slices.

"We do have something we have to admit to the officer though," Leila said.

"It's true," said Eva. "I hope you won't think we were too much of a busybody, but it seemed right at the time."

"What is it?" asked Heather.

"We ran into Rudolph Rodney, and so we told him to go to Donut Delights in the morning. We thought maybe you both should have an official meeting with him to get more details so you can make your decision," Eva said. "I'm sorry if this was overstepping."

"It's all right," Heather said. "I think a meeting with him is exactly what we need."

"Really?" Lilly asked, smiling. "Because I think pizza and donuts are exactly what we need."

Chapter 15

"I normally don't like mixing business with pleasure," Rudolph Rodney said. "But when it comes to these donuts, I just can't help myself."

"I understand the sentiment," Heather said.

She was pleased that she was able to call in her reinforcements for the meeting so quickly. She joined Rudolph Rodney at the table with Ryan and Col. Lilly was in the shop, but was letting the adults have their important discussion. Instead, Lilly was helping Heather's assistants Angelica and Maricela as they served up some more of the week's special flavors.

"And speaking with you all is looking like it is going to be a real pleasure too," said Rudolph. "Now should we get down to the nuts and bolts of the icing and sprinkles?"

"I think that's a good idea," Heather said.

"I hope you don't mind," Ryan said. "But I am a detective. I did a little digging on you. Everything seems to be in order."

"I don't mind at all," Rudolph Rodney said. "And I did a little research on this place myself. I didn't just let my taste buds guide my judgment. But it all just makes me more excited to make a deal."

"We want to make sure that this business deal is in the best interest of Donut Delights," Col said. "As well as for the Shepherds and their family."

"I understand. I think we can find a deal that will be mutually beneficial," Rudolph said, nodding. "As I mentioned before, I have a storefront on Duval Street. It is a prime location in Key West, and I have been waiting for the right business to set up there. I don't believe it would be an issue to set up the kitchens or front of house in the space. My immediate thoughts on the deal would be that I provide the location and initial set up of the space. Heather will provide the recipes and training to the staff. Then we can find an agreeable way to split the profits, of which I'm sure there will be plenty to go around."

"I like what we are both bringing to the table," said Heather.

"I am preparing all aspects of the space," Rudolph said. "But she is bringing the heart and soul. And I'd like to have her there for at least a year to make sure that everything is running smoothly and that it is a true Donut Delights there."

"We'd have to discuss the online ordering aspect of the business," Col said. "Both how filling the orders would be split between the two locations and how profits would be divided."

"Col has already helped the online business grow as my joint venture partner," Heather said.

"Perhaps we should discuss having some of your specialty teas at the new location," Rudolph Rodney said. "If that's beneficial to both of you. Of course, I'm going to have to taste it first."

"You won't be disappointed with any of the flavors from either of these two," Ryan assured him.

Maricela brought over another dish of donuts for the table. She had a curious expression on her face. She knew something important was going on, but politely left after delivering the food and napkins. Heather felt sure that she was going to be bombarded with questions later and hoped that she would have good answers for them.

The business meeting paused for a moment as everyone took another donut.

"I'm so happy to become a part of this tasty business," Rudolph Rodney said.

"Now you said you had houses too?" Heather prodded.

"Yes," Rudolph said. "As part of my bribe to get you to move down there, I'm offering several properties for you to stay at. I'll show you the options I have, and I would allow your family to have it rent free for the year. I've been very picky about who I let rent and have allowed them to stay empty for too long. I won't be losing any money with this offer, especially as donut business picks up."

"That is a wonderful perk," Ryan said.

"We have to look into the area to make sure that other aspects of our lives will fit in there too," Heather said. "But how about we finish this round of donuts, and then get into negotiations about profits?"

They all agreed that seemed like a sound plan. Heather reached for a napkin that she thought would be necessary with all the chocolate she was about to eat, but the napkin caught on the table and tore.

The others at the table had begun chatting again, but

Heather became absorbed with the napkin. A thought occurred to her, and she tore it again. The rest of the business meeting turned to her as she grabbed another napkin and tore it to shreds. She looked at the uneven pieces that had fallen into her lap. She stood up quickly and let them fall to the floor.

"I'm sorry, Maricela, that you'll have to clean that up," Heather said. "I need to go."

"Where?" Rudolph asked.

"Please continue this meeting," Heather said. "You're some of the people I trust the most, and I want to see this move forward.

But I need to go and check something now. I think I just discovered who the murderer is."

Chapter 16

Heather looked at the bagged fabric in evidence that Hoskins had allowed her to examine. It looked like her hunch was right.

"But is there enough evidence to prove it?" she asked herself.

"What was that?" Amy asked, joining her in the room.

"Ames, I'm so glad you're here."

"Are you really?" she said, crossing her arms. "Because it seems like you're leaving me out of the loop."

"I called you as soon as I figured out this clue in the case," Heather said.

"Not the case. You think I care about the case?" Amy said, "Well, maybe I do care about the case, but that's not what I'm talking about. Your meeting with Roadkill's uncle about moving away. Were you going to tell me about it?"

"Yes. I was trying to get more information to see if it's worth going."

"You already know the answer," Amy said. "Don't go. Everything is here. Everyone is here."

"Amy, if I did move, you know that you'd still be my best friend," Heather started.

"You're not acting like a best friend," Amy snapped.

"Well, neither are you," Heather said. "I might have been presented with an amazing opportunity. But all you're doing is trying to belittle it and me."

"I just moved in with Jamie," Amy said suddenly. "Why did you have to wait until I couldn't follow to go?"

"You know I didn't plan this," Heather said.

"And you'd be leaving Mona and her wedding."

"I'd be here for the wedding, and I'd still help," Heather insisted.

"What if Jamie and I get engaged?" Amy asked.

"Then I'd come back and help with that too."

"You can't be Maid of Honor from across the country," Amy said. "I hate that you're abandoning me. Things finally seemed to be going right."

Heather was about to respond, but instead asked, "Are you mad right now?"

"Duh," Amy said. "Did we grow so far apart that you can't tell?"

"If you're angry, tear apart this fabric," Heather said, handing her a large scrap she had carried in her purse.

Amy obliged and tore the fabric into pieces.

"Actually," Amy said. "That was stress relieving. Do you have any more?"

"No," Heather said. "But look at the pieces."

"What am I looking at?" Amy asked, staring at the mess.

"You were angry and were just destroying the fabric because it was there."

"And because you told me to," Amy said. "Don't try and make me sound like a crazy person."

"Your rips and tears are all uneven."

"So?"

"So, look at the fabric pieces that were found at the crime scene. They're all about the same length. One foot. I didn't think it was strange at the time, but now these tears look deliberate."

"They weren't made in the heat of the moment in anger," Amy said. "They were done to set the scene."

"Exactly," said Heather. "The killer made it look like someone angry about their dress and wedding killed Sheila Lordlittle out of revenge, but this was just to distract us."

"It almost worked," said Amy.

"I think that the fabric being ripped into similar sizes tells us something else," said Heather. "I think it tells us that the killer works with fabric a lot and knows how to use it."

"One of the sewing assistants," Amy said. "Ollie or Abigail."

"I'm even more grateful for my current staff," Heather said. "No murderers working for me right now. I'm sorry I left such a mess for Maricela to clean up though."

"Which of them did it?" Amy wondered aloud. "Ollie found the body, but could that be cover up? And neither had good alibis."

"Something else started to bother me," Heather said. "Do you remember what June Grady told us?"

"Yes," Amy said. "And I promise if I ever get engaged not to turn into a Bridezilla who drives everyone including the groom away."

"Abigail Browning said that she couldn't remember the names of the unhappy customers and that's why she wrote down the description of the dresses," Heather said.

"Yes," said Amy. "But that makes sense. There are some customers at Donut Delights that I don't know the names of, but I know the order for. That one lady that always gets the fruit flavored donut. And the guy who always gets one donut to eat in the shop and then gets a repeat one for the road."

"It does make sense. But there's a problem too. Do you remember what June Grady said about her having a nickname?"

"The staff called her a Grady A Nightmare," Amy said. "That is a great insulting nickname."

"It was based on her name," Heather said. "I think it's unlikely that they would have forgotten her name when asked about unhappy customers."
"But why would Abigail cover that up?" Amy asked.

"I think," Heather said. "Because I asked her to write it down."

Realization dawned on Amy's face. "She wrote on the wall and didn't want her handwriting matched."

"Ryan was right that it would be hard to match writing from paper to the wall. People could hold the writing utensil differently. But the "g" in "something" was distinctive," Heather said. "Remember how I said it looked curly?"

"It was really curly," Amy agreed. "So?"

"So, when Abigail wrote down the list of potential suspects, she avoided using the letter G. Now that I think about it, she avoided using it a lot. There was Tabitha Greenwald, Holly Lag, Betsy Gene and June Grady. Every one of them had a G in their last name."

"So, we found our killer!" Amy said.

"I think so," Heather said. "But do we have enough evidence to prove it?"

Chapter 17

"Should we wait for Ryan?" Amy asked.

"I don't think so," Heather said. "He's on his way, but there's no reason not to start."

She and Amy entered Lordlittle's Lovely Gowns. It looked even creepier than the last time they were there. The dresses that were torn had been removed from the scene, but the threatening message was still scrawled ominously. Having only part of the scene intact somehow looked even more threatening.

"Okay, I have a reason," Amy said. "This is seriously creepy. And what are we even looking for?"

"Any piece of evidence that might have been overlooked," Heather said. "Hopefully, we'll know it when we see it."

They looked amongst the dresses that were still hanging in the shop. Then they moved into the back room. A long table had fabric spread out on it, and there were three sewing machines that were set up.

The friends split up and began looking for evidence.

"I think I found something," Heather said.

Amy hurried over and she showed her the book that she had found. It was Abigail's sketchbook, containing designs of several dresses. It also had her name written on the inside cover.

"This "g" in "Abigail" looks an awful lot like what was written on the wall, don't you think?" said Heather.

Amy nodded and looked through the book. "It's a shame she's a killer," she said. "These dresses are pretty nice looking."

"Thanks," a voice said. "I'll be taking that book if you don't mind."

They saw Abigail entering the room.

"Actually, we do mind," Amy said, clutching the book close to her. "This is evidence now."

"It's my personal property, and I want it back."

"Is that why you're here?" Heather asked. "To get this sketchbook?"

"I thought it would be safe to get it now. I never meant to leave it behind. It has all my ideas inside," Abigail said. "Now give it to me."

Instead, Heather and Amy made a run for the doorway. Amy made it farther with the sketchbook, but Abigail caught up with Heather. She grabbed Heather's hair and pulled her back. Then she picked up a pair of sewing shears from a workbench and threatened Heather with them.

"Give me the sketchbook or your friend isn't making it out of here alive," Abigail said.

Heather couldn't fight back with Abigail holding the shears so close to her throat. She looked around the room. An iron was nearby, but it was too risky to move with the sharp shears ready to attack.

Amy paused. "How would you explain that to the police?" she asked stalling.

"I guess I'd have to say that she died trying to save me from the same crazed killer that got Ms. Lordlittle," Abigail said. "Now give me the sketchbook."

"Why did you kill Ms. Lordlittle?" Amy asked.

"She wouldn't even look at my sketches," Abigail said. "She was making the most ridiculous things, but wouldn't look at my designs. What was the point of working here if I couldn't move up? This was hurting my career. And so, I wanted to hurt her."

"And after you killed her, you set the scene to look like an unhappy bride attacked her?" Amy asked.

"How did you know it was me?" Abigail asked. "My handwriting? I thought I was so careful."

"And the rips you made in the dresses," Amy said. "They were too professionally done."

Heather tried to join in. "You said you didn't recognize the dress fabric that was used to strangle her, but it had to have come from the store. You grabbed it because it was easily accessible, but then pretended you hadn't seen it recently. You wanted us to think that it was from the unhappy bride's wedding."

Abigail was tired of talking. She adjusted her grip on Heather and moved the shears closer. "Give me the sketchbook," she repeated.

Amy locked eyes with Heather, and then Heather looked at the iron. Without speaking, they formed a plan.

"I have a better idea," Amy said. "Let Heather go, or I'll tear your designs to shreds."

She opened the book to emphasize her threat. In horror, Abigail loosened her hold on Heather.

Heather moved quickly. She grabbed the iron and hit Abigail with it, then she and Amy ran out of the shop as quickly as they could.

They were just catching their breath outside when Ryan appeared on the scene. They explained what happened and Ryan rushed inside to capture the killer.

The two friends were just happy that this case didn't turn out to be their last.

Chapter 18

"You were almost killed," Amy said. "What am I going to do if you get yourself killed?"

"I'll try not to let it happen," Heather assured her.

They were both in stalls in a new dress shop, trying on bridesmaid dresses. It sounded as if they were about to have a touching moment, and Heather found it amusing that they were discussing it through a wall.

"That's what I worry about," Amy said. "If you move away, who's going to have your back when you get into trouble with killers?"

"I'd be moving to start another donut shop," Heather said. "Not as an investigator."

"Yeah, but how long is that going to last. Sleuthing is in your blood. You're not going to be able to give it up for long," Amy said. "And besides, the last time we went to Key West, and on vacation, mind you, we ended up involved in a murder case."

Heather had to admit that she had a point there.

"I'd be careful," Heather said.

"I know," Amy said. "And I know you can take care of yourself. But you're my best friend. I don't want anything bad to happen to you. Especially if I'm not there to help."

"I understand," Heather said. "I'd be worried about you solving cases in Hillside on your on too. But I know you can handle it."

"Solve cases on my own?" Amy asked.

"Were you going to retire without me?" Heather asked.

"I hadn't really thought about it," Amy admitted.

"You shouldn't give it up. You have a gift for it too. And," said

Heather. "Who was the one who saved me from the killer?"

"I guess I am pretty good at what I do," Amy said.

Heather finished zipping up her dress and started to emerge from her stall.

"I really am happy for you, and I want you to do what's best for you," Amy said. "I'd just miss you so much."

Amy emerged from her stall too, and the two friends hugged. Mona joined them and grinned at what she saw.

"Everyone is feeling the love?" she asked.

"I guess so," said Amy.

They stepped back, and all looked at the new bridesmaid dresses. They were flattering on both of the co-Maids of Honor. They were pink like the roses that Mona had been fond of. While pink didn't always compliment Heather's hair, this shade actually looked stunning on her.

"I think these might be the dresses I want," Mona said. "They look beautiful on you both."

"Really?" Amy joked. "I was leaning towards that first one that I tried on with all the ruffles."

"Don't tease," Mona said. "I could still bring that one back."

However, as they looked into the mirror, they knew that these pink dresses were the right choice for Mona's wedding. They were elegant and cozy at the same time.

"Now, Heather, Col was so excited about this Florida deal, he can't seem to stop talking about it. And it's making me excited about it too. But you've got to promise me that you'll still help me with my wedding plans."

"Of course, I promise," Heather said.

"Good," Mona said. "Because I need both of you."

"You couldn't stop us if you tried," Amy said.

"And now that we've found these bridesmaid dresses are we set with the dresses?" Heather asked. "Or are we back to square one with the wedding dress?"

"The police told me that I could have the dress if I want it. It's no longer a piece of evidence," Mona said. "And I think Sheila Lordlittle would like it if I wore what she designed."

"But how do you feel about it?" asked Heather.

"I still think it's the perfect dress," Mona said. "Even if the circumstances surrounding it weren't ideal, it's what's right for me. I'm excited to wear it on my wedding day."

Heather's heart felt light as she stood there with her friends. Mona's words rang true. Mona had made peace with her thoughts that she and Col weren't meant to be together. She realized that even though wedding planning had not been ideal, they were still in love and were going to make the wedding and marriage work. Heather felt similar about her move. She hadn't been expecting it and leaving her friends was not going to be ideal, but it seemed like the right choice for her. She was excited for the changes that it would bring, but for today, she was happy to be with her friends in a pretty dress.

The End

A letter from the Author

To each and every one of my Amazing readers: *I hope you enjoyed this story as much as I enjoyed writing it. Let me know what you think by leaving a review!*

Stay Curious,
Susan Gillard

Made in the USA
Middletown, DE
18 August 2017